YOU AND YOUR CHILD
ODDS & ENDS

Ray Gibson

Illustrated by Sue Stitt, Simone Abel
and Graham Round

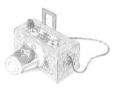

Designed by Carol Law
Edited by Robyn Gee
Series editor: Jenny Tyler

Photography by Lesley Howling

There is a great variety of things you can make using odds and ends from around the house. This book is designed to give you some ideas and starting points. Besides providing enjoyment and satisfaction, this type of activity can help young children to develop skills such as hand control and co-ordination, concentration and decision-making, and broaden their understanding of concepts such as size, shape, space and measurement.

Post box

Poke a hole in each corner with a ball-point pen before you start cutting.

Use a felt-tip pen to draw a door on the back of a large box. Cut three sides with a breadknife.

Stick on a bottle cap to make a handle.

Crease gently down side four with the knife. Fold the door outward to make a hinge.

On the front, draw and cut out a slit large enough for letters.

Other ideas to try:

Parcels

Wrap a variety of small empty boxes and toys to mail, using old wrapping paper, cellophane tape and string.
   Glue on addresses cut from old letters.

Letters

Save old envelopes, postcards and birthday cards for your mail bag.

Postbag

Use an old shopping bag or big shoulder bag.

POST OFFICE

Pour some paint into a bowl and paint the box. When the paint has dried, add patterns and a label using a felt-tip pen.

Ink-pad and franking stamp

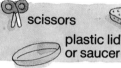
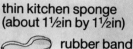

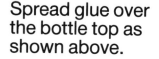
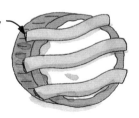

Trim away any excess with scissors.

Spread glue over the bottle top as shown above.

Lay pieces of rubber band onto the glue.

Place a piece of damp sponge in the plastic lid.

Pour a little paint into the center of the sponge.

Press the bottle top into the paint and print firmly over the stamps (see right).

Stamps

Use an unthreaded sewing machine to perforate squares of gummed paper. Draw a simple design on each stamp.

You could also use redemption stamps.

Other ideas to try

Counter holder

Cut empty cereal boxes down to different heights. Glue them together in order of size. Stock with postcards, licenses and birthday cards to sell.

Add a cardboard tube for holding pens and pencils.

Cash box and money

Use a plastic ice cream box to hold play money.

Make your own money by cutting dollars out of paper.

For coins, use washed and flattened foil bottle tops.

Add a toy telephone and some kitchen scales on which to weigh parcels.

Camera and photos

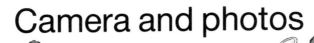

You will need: scissors glue large toothpaste cap small plastic carton or cup

small hinge-lid box (e.g. tea-bag box) ball-point pen 30in yarn or plastic packaging tape pictures cut from magazines or newspapers, or squares of plain paper

cellophane tape piece of thin cardboard (1½in by 2in) piece of plastic wrap (1½in by 2in)

Assemble your camera as shown below.

For a press button, glue a toothpaste cap to the top of the box.

Glue the viewfinder to the top back of the box.

To make the viewfinder, cut out the center of a piece of cardboard, as shown. Stick the plastic wrap over it, then glue it to the top of the box.

Use a ball-point pen to poke holes in either side of the box for a strap.
Thread the tape or yarn through and knot on the inside.

Have the hinge of the lid at the top front of the box.

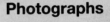

Hints

If you use yarn for the strap, you can stiffen the ends with cellophane tape to make it easier to thread through the holes.

Remember to take into account whether the photographer is right or left-handed before glueing on the press button.

Glue the plastic carton or cup to the center front of the box to look like a lens.

Photographs

Cut small pictures from magazines or newspapers, or draw some pictures on squares of paper.
Keep the "photographs" inside the box.

Binoculars

You will need:

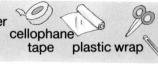
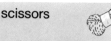
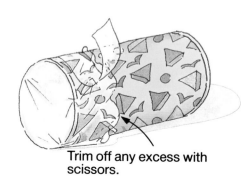

2 toilet paper tubes

wrapping paper

cellophane tape

plastic wrap

scissors

ball-point pen

30in yarn

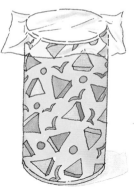

Trim off any excess with scissors.

Cut a piece of wrapping paper to cover each toilet paper tube. Secure it with cellophane tape.

Cut a piece of plastic wrap to cover the end of each toilet paper tube. Tape it in place.

Use a ball-point pen to poke two holes for the straps.

Thread yarn through the holes. Tie knots in the ends to secure it.

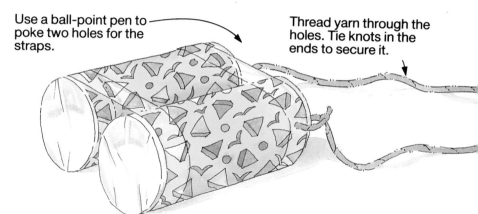

Hints

If you have no toilet paper tubes, cut up a paper towel tube using a breadknife as a saw.

When using cellophane tape, cut the required number of strips and attach them lightly to your work surface ready for use.

Use microwave plastic wrap for easier handling.

Secure the tubes firmly together using two strips of cellophane tape.

Other ideas to try

Walkie-talkie

Wrap an 8oz juice carton in paper, as you would wrap a small parcel. Use a straw as an aerial.
  Stick on squares of gummed paper for buttons and write numbers on them.

Colored flashlight

Change the color of a flashlight beam by securing colored cellophane over the glass with a rubber band.

Magic telescope

Tape colored cellophane over a paper towel tube, so that everything looks a different color.

Moon rocket

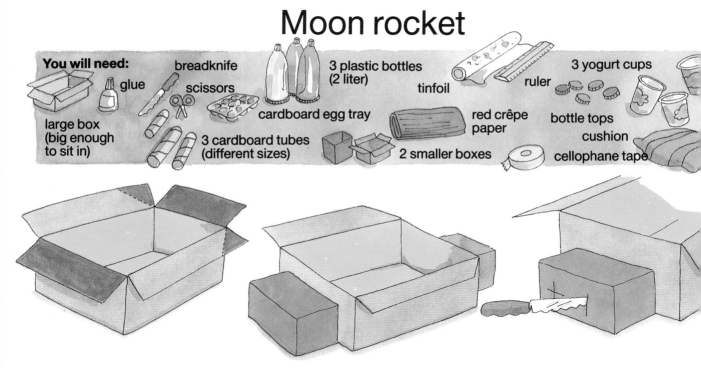

You will need:
glue · breadknife · scissors · 3 plastic bottles (2 liter) · tinfoil · ruler · 3 yogurt cups · large box (big enough to sit in) · 3 cardboard tubes (different sizes) · cardboard egg tray · red crêpe paper · bottle tops · cushion · 2 smaller boxes · cellophane tape

Using a breadknife, cut off the parts of the large box shaded dark brown in the picture above.

Use glue and cellophane tape to attach the smaller boxes to the front and back, to make a nose and a fuel tank.

Cut two crosses 1½in by 1½in in the back of the fuel tank, using the tip of the breadknife.

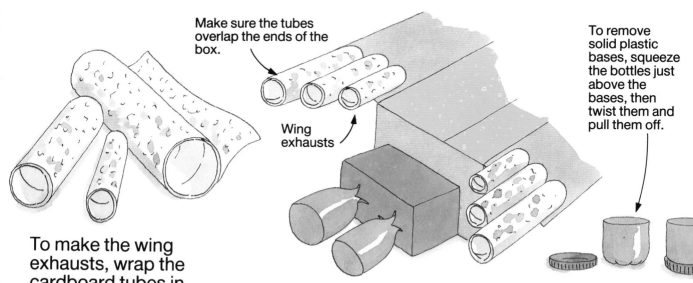

Make sure the tubes overlap the ends of the box.

Wing exhausts

To remove solid plastic bases, squeeze the bottles just above the bases, then twist them and pull them off.

To make the wing exhausts, wrap the cardboard tubes in tinfoil, securing it with tape. Cut each tube in half. Glue the tubes onto the wings as shown.

To make the tail exhausts, cut the bottoms off the bottles about 3½in from the base. Insert two of the bottle necks firmly into the crosses cut in the fuel tank. You will need the bases later.

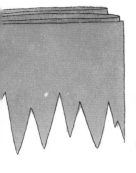
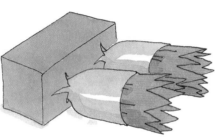

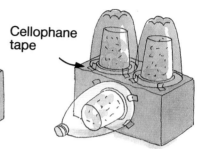

Fold a piece of crêpe paper and cut a jagged edge so that it looks like flames. Cut it into two pieces. Roll each piece loosely and bunch it into the bottles. Secure it with sticky tape.

For lights, cover yogurt cups with tinfoil. Glue two cups on top of the nose and a third on the front.

Tape the remaining cut bottle and two bottle bases over them.

Cellophane tape

Control panel

Cover an egg tray with tinfoil, pressing gently into the hollows.

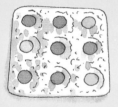

Glue bottle tops in the hollows to make press buttons.

Attach the panel to the inside front of the spaceship.

Add a cushion for the pilot to sit on.

Use an empty liquid soap container as a can for spare fuel.

Hints

If you don't have all the things listed, you can easily improvise on the basic shape with such things as jar lids, polystyrene packaging and plastic food trays.

For a larger spaceship, glue a second box between the main body and the fuel tank.

For extra decoration, cover the solid plastic bottle bases with foil and stick them onto the wings and fuel tank.

7

Caravan

You will need: very large box (for refrigerator, cooker or something similar) breadknife large, thin book felt-tip pen large bottle cap cellophane tape ruler scissors

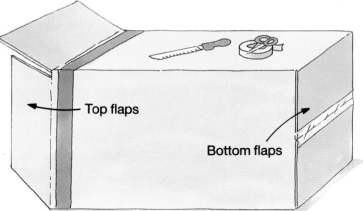

Top flaps

Bottom flaps

Lay the box on its side and cut off any top flaps, using a breadknife. Use cellophane tape to close the bottom flaps firmly.

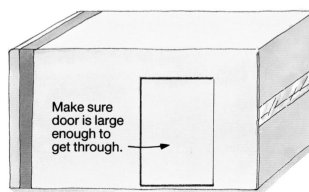

Make sure door is large enough to get through.

Using a ruler, draw a door shape large enough for your child to get through. Cut around three sides and bend it outward to make a door.

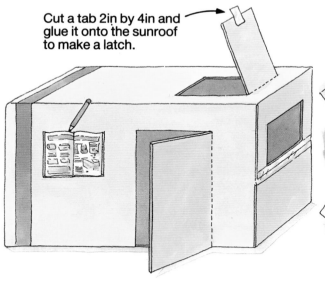

Cut a tab 2in by 4in and glue it onto the sunroof to make a latch.

To make the windows, draw around a thin, open book, then cut around the lines with a breadknife.

Place the book on the roof and draw around it. Cut around three sides and bend the flap up to make a sunroof.

Stick tape across the corners first.

Cut pieces of plastic wrap larger than the open book and use cellophane tape to attach them over the inside of the windows.

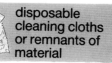
disposable cleaning cloths or remnants of material

glue

plastic wrap

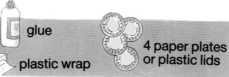
4 paper plates or plastic lids

Other ideas to try:

Make a small caravan for a doll or teddy. Choose a box it can fit inside.

Make a tiny caravan from a very small box. Attach it to a toy car, using string or cellophane tape.

Make folds along the top of the material.

Cut strips of material and tape them to the top inside edges of the windows for curtains.

Put a small box inside to make a table and a cushion for a seat. Add a flashlight, plastic cups and a drink in a plastic bottle.

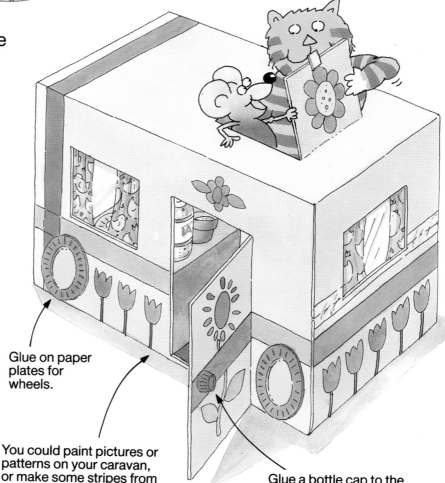

Hint

Turn the box so whichever side you are working on is at the top.

Glue on paper plates for wheels.

You could paint pictures or patterns on your caravan, or make some stripes from colored cellophane tape.

Glue a bottle cap to the door to make a handle.

Airport and heliport

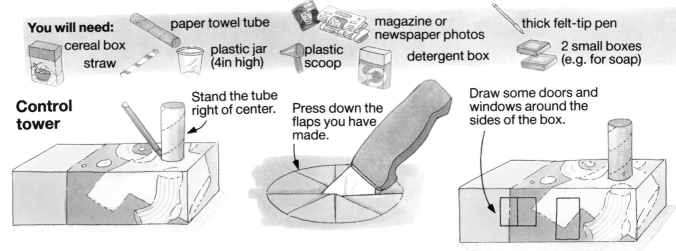

You will need: cereal box, paper towel tube, straw, plastic jar (4in high), plastic scoop, magazine or newspaper photos, detergent box, thick felt-tip pen, 2 small boxes (e.g. for soap)

Control tower

Stand the tube right of center.

Press down the flaps you have made.

Draw some doors and windows around the sides of the box.

Stand the paper towel tube on the detergent box, as shown, and draw around it with a felt-tip pen.

Poke a slit in the center of the circle. Cut to the edge, using a breadknife. Make cuts all the way round, as shown.

Push the paper towel firmly into the hole so that it stands upright.

Helicopter pad

If you don't have a plastic jar, use a breadknife to cut off a clear, plastic bottle.

Cut some pictures of people from magazine photographs. Glue them onto the inside of the upturned plastic jar.

Put plenty of glue around the top of the paper towel tube. Press the plastic jar firmly on top.

Remove the lid from a pizza box and turn the box upside down.
　Draw around a jar lid to make a large circle in the center. Write a large "H" for helicopter in the circle.

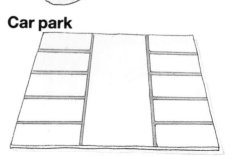

Materials

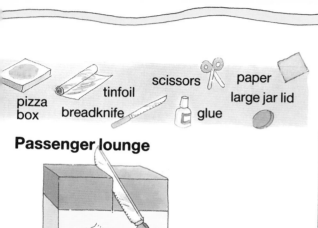

pizza box, tinfoil, breadknife, scissors, glue, paper, large jar lid

Passenger lounge

Saw a cereal box in half lengthways, using a breadknife. Turn one half on its side and glue it onto the left of the control tower base.

Attach a small box on top of it to make a look-out point. Make a hole in the small box, push in a straw and stick on a paper flag.

Car park

Remove the flaps from the pizza box lid. Draw car spaces on the lid and put it in front of the control tower.

Radar

Push the handle of a scoop into a small box and glue the box to the top of the control tower building.

Runway

Using scissors, cut away the side panel from the remaining half of the cereal box. Open out the box to make a flat strip.

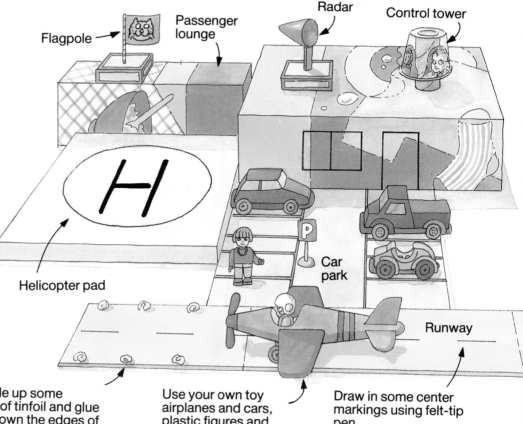

Flagpole

Passenger lounge

Radar

Control tower

Helicopter pad

Car park

Runway

Crumple up some pieces of tinfoil and glue them down the edges of the runway for lights.

Use your own toy airplanes and cars, plastic figures and traffic signs.

Draw in some center markings using felt-tip pen.

Pull-along train

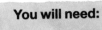
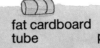

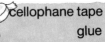
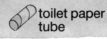
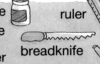

You will need:

long box with low sides (approx. 6in high) (box 1)

2 smaller boxes, narrower than box 1 (boxes 2 and 3)

even smaller box (box 4)

fat cardboard tube

plastic tub

toilet paper tube

cellophane tape

glue

breadknife

ruler

ball-point pen

Engine base

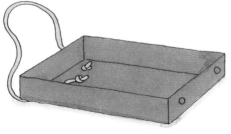

Turn box 1 over to form a base. Using a ball-point pen, poke four holes, as shown above.

Cut a piece of clothes line about 6ft long. Poke the ends through the top holes and knot them inside the box.

Cut another piece of clothes line about 28in long. Thread it through the back holes and leave the ends free.

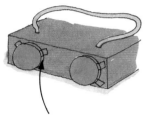
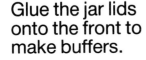

Hold in place with cellophane tape.

Glue the jar lids onto the front to make buffers.

Cabin

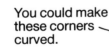

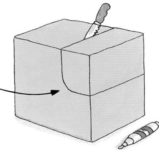

You could make these corners curved.

On box 2, draw lines as shown above, using a ruler and a felt-tip pen. Cut along the lines with a breadknife.

Using a plastic tub as a pattern, draw a circle in the top front left-hand corner. Make a hole in the center of the circle, using a ball-point pen.

Insert the breadknife, cut to the edge, then round the outline of the circle. Remove the circle to make a window for the driver.

Glue the cabin to the back end of the base. Use cellophane tape for extra strength.

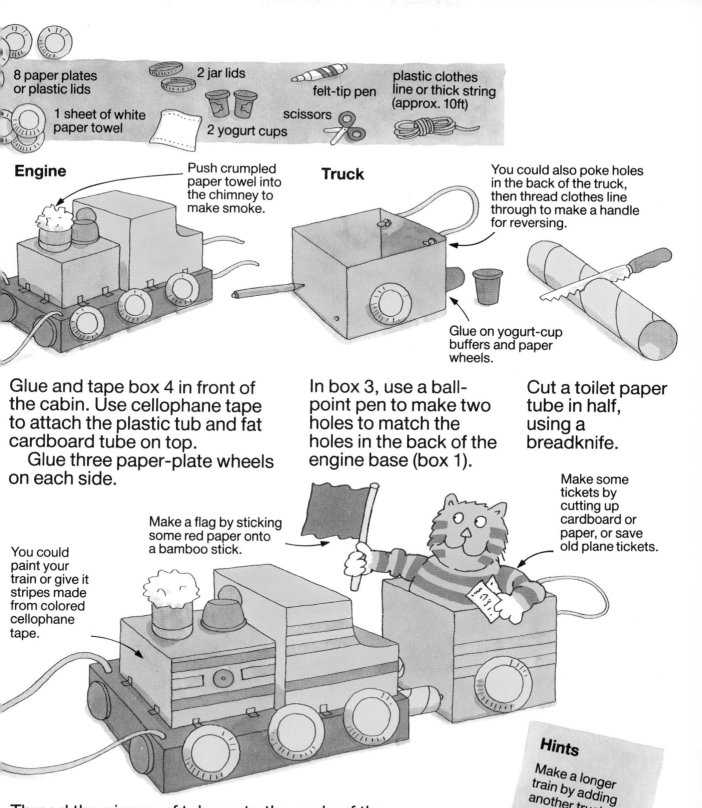

8 paper plates or plastic lids

2 jar lids

felt-tip pen

plastic clothes line or thick string (approx. 10ft)

1 sheet of white paper towel

2 yogurt cups

scissors

Engine

Push crumpled paper towel into the chimney to make smoke.

Truck

You could also poke holes in the back of the truck, then thread clothes line through to make a handle for reversing.

Glue on yogurt-cup buffers and paper wheels.

Glue and tape box 4 in front of the cabin. Use cellophane tape to attach the plastic tub and fat cardboard tube on top.

Glue three paper-plate wheels on each side.

In box 3, use a ball-point pen to make two holes to match the holes in the back of the engine base (box 1).

Cut a toilet paper tube in half, using a breadknife.

Make some tickets by cutting up cardboard or paper, or save old plane tickets.

Make a flag by sticking some red paper onto a bamboo stick.

You could paint your train or give it stripes made from colored cellophane tape.

Thread the pieces of tube onto the ends of the clothes line at the back of the engine base. Then thread the ends through the holes at the front of the truck and tie them in a knot.

Hints

Make a longer train by adding another truck or a guard's van and attaching it in the same way.

13

Dog kennel

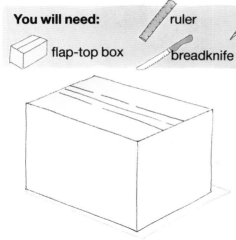

You will need: ruler, ball-point pen, cellophane tape, scissors, newspaper, flap-top box, breadknife, saucer, felt-tip pen, powder paint, corrugated cardboard, paintbrush

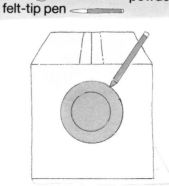

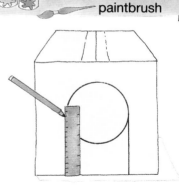

Stick the top flaps of the box down with tape. If necessary, do the same with the bottom flaps.

Place a saucer on the center front of the box and draw around it with a felt-tip pen.

Using a ruler, draw two lines from the sides of the circle to the bottom edge of the box.

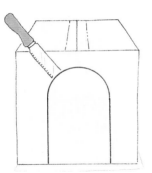

Using a breadknife, cut around the arch-shape to make a doorway. To insert the knife, first make a hole with a ball-point pen.

Place the box on an old newspaper to paint it.

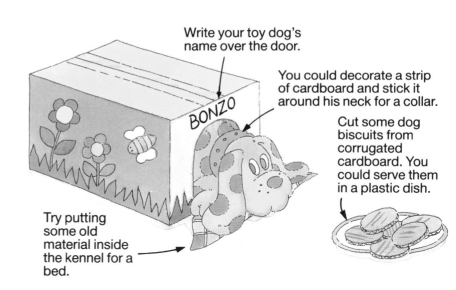

Write your toy dog's name over the door.

You could decorate a strip of cardboard and stick it around his neck for a collar.

Cut some dog biscuits from corrugated cardboard. You could serve them in a plastic dish.

BONZO

Try putting some old material inside the kennel for a bed.

Another idea to try
Cat basket

Using a ruler, draw a line around a box about 4in from the base. Cut off the top using a breadknife.

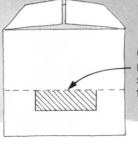

Cut a rectangular section from the front.

Paint the outside of the box and put a cushion inside for your toy cat to sit on.

Tying and threading trays

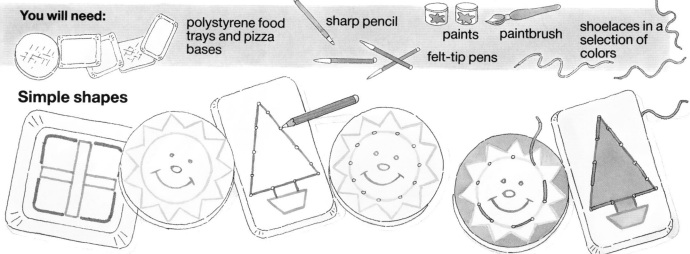

You will need: polystyrene food trays and pizza bases — sharp pencil — paints — paintbrush — felt-tip pens — shoelaces in a selection of colors

Simple shapes

Draw some large, simple shapes on the back of food trays, using felt-tip pens. You will need to press firmly.

Poke holes at intervals around the main outline, using a pencil with a sharp point.

Paint the shapes. Thread around the outline with laces.

Random patterns

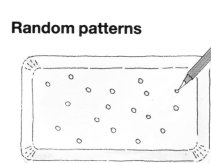

If possible use several colors.

Use a sharp pencil to poke holes through a food tray from the back.

Use the tray for threading criss-cross patterns with shoelaces.

Shoe-laces

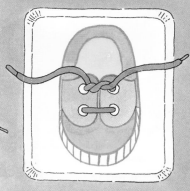

Draw and paint a shoe. Poke lace-holes in it.

Use the shoe to practice tying knots and bows.

Other ideas to try

Sewing on buttons

Use scissors to cut the bases off two clean, dry polystyrene cups about ½in from the bottom. Poke two holes in each, using a sharp pencil.

Draw and color a clown on a food tray or a piece of cardboard. Place the buttons on him and make four holes in the tray or cardboard to correspond with the button holes.

"Sew" on the buttons with shoelaces.

Fleet of boats

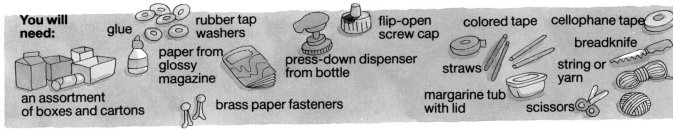
Police launch

Cut a clean dry milk carton in half lengthways.

Cut off a light-bulb box and tape it into the center of one half of the milk carton.

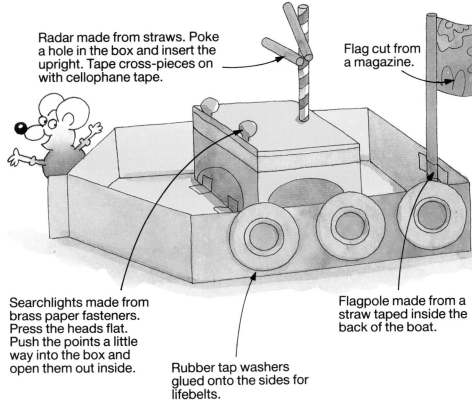

Radar made from straws. Poke a hole in the box and insert the upright. Tape cross-pieces on with cellophane tape.

Flag cut from a magazine.

Searchlights made from brass paper fasteners. Press the heads flat. Push the points a little way into the box and open them out inside.

Rubber tap washers glued onto the sides for lifebelts.

Flagpole made from a straw taped inside the back of the boat.

Tugboat

Trim the bows slightly with scissors.

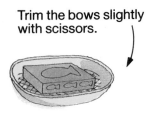

Glue a flat box (e.g. a sardine box) onto the base of a polystyrene food tray.

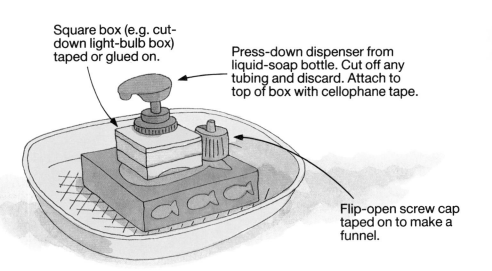

Square box (e.g. cut-down light-bulb box) taped or glued on.

Press-down dispenser from liquid-soap bottle. Cut off any tubing and discard. Attach to top of box with cellophane tape.

Flip-open screw cap taped on to make a funnel.

Other ideas to try

Hovercraft

Fins cut from cardboard, colored and slotted into slits made with a breadknife.

Glue paper circles onto cut-down straws to make rotors.

Upside-down margarine tub with lid.

Make holes with sharp scissors and push the straws in.

Colored tape

Catamaran

Magazine paper taped onto straw mast.

Sardine box

Toothpaste tube boxes.

Barges

Toilet paper tube for cabin.

Long thin box (e.g. for cookies)

Corks for cargo. You could also use twigs, matchboxes and raisin boxes.

Join the small barges to the big one by taping on string.

Matchbox center

Bath-salt coal

Hints

Polystyrene packaging blocks make a good base for boats.

Assemble the cabins completely before attaching them to their bases.

Submarines

For submarines use shampoo bottles with various levels of water to float at different heights in the bath.

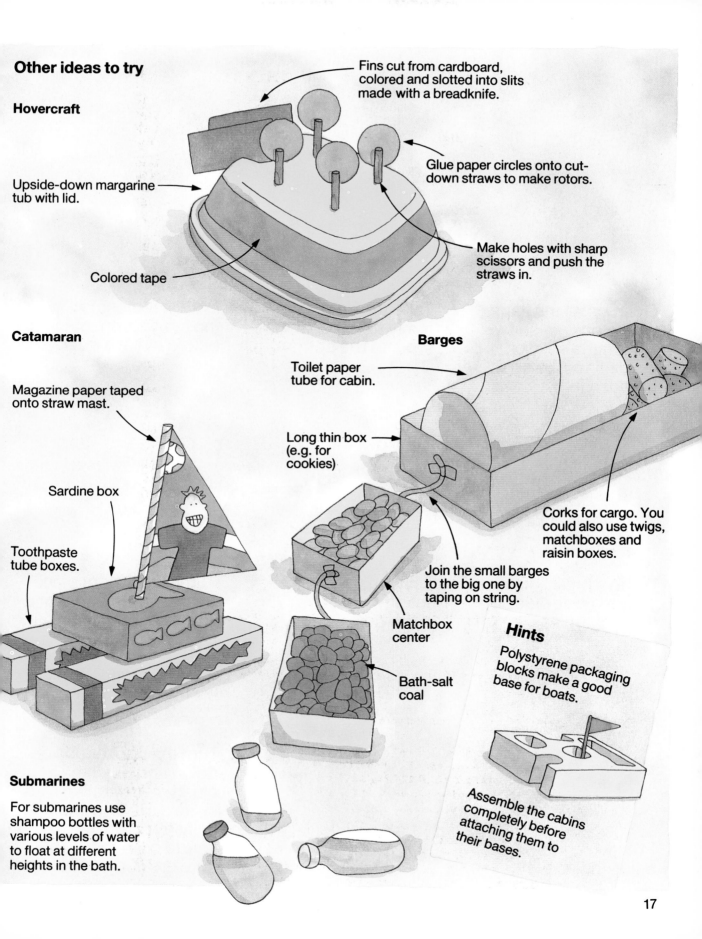

Cooker

You will need: large box · breadknife · ruler · tinfoil · large screw-top bottle cap · 4 plastic tub or jar lids · glue · 5 small bottle caps · scissors · cellophane tape · felt-tip pen

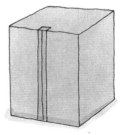

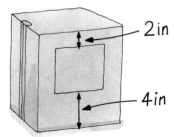

2 in

4 in

Smaller flap

Open up all the flaps on the box, as shown. Cut off the smaller, inside flaps, using a breadknife.

Tape the outer flaps firmly together at the top and the bottom.

Draw a rectangle on the center front of the box to make a door.

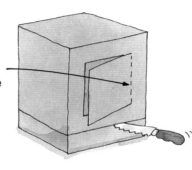

Fold back to make a hinge down the fourth side.

Using a breadknife, cut around three sides of the rectangle.

Using the breadknife, cut off the bottom 2in of the box.

Turn this bottom piece upside down and trim a ½in strip from the front.

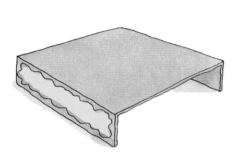

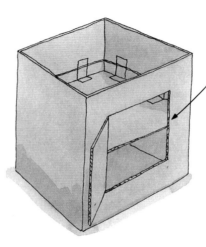

Make sure the trimmed edge of the shelf is at the front.

Put glue on the three sides that are left.

Turn the cooker upside down and push the glued piece firmly inside to form a shelf halfway down.

Add cellophane tape for extra support.

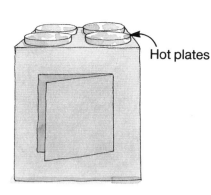
Hot plates

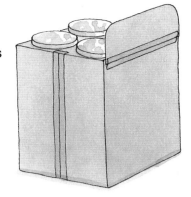

Cover jar lids with pieces of tinfoil and tape them to the top of the cooker.

Cut a strip of cardboard 3in deep, round off the top corners and tape it to the top back of the cooker.

Other ideas to try

Refrigerator

Make as for the cooker, but leave out the hot plates and control knobs.

Fill with:

empty, washed-out milk cartons

egg boxes

playdough butter and cheese on paper plates or jar lids

crumpled tinfoil fish

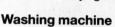

margarine and yogurt tubs

Washing machine

Draw around a circular 1 quart ice cream tub on the center front of a large box. Use a breadknife to cut almost around the circle, but leave a hinge at the side. Glue and tape the lid of the tub onto the door.

Cut a flap on top for soap powder.

Add a large screw-on bottle cap as the programming dial.

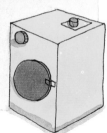

To go with your cooker:

Use plastic margarine tubs as pans or mixing bowls.

Draw on a clock face.

Make food from playdough using a rolling pin and plastic cutters.

Use playdough to ice an upside-down margarine-tub cake on a paper plate. Add pasta shells as decoration

Refrigerator. (See Other ideas to try, on the right.)

Glue and tape on bottle-cap knobs. Glue and tape on a screw-top door handle.

Borrow an apron and oven gloves from the kitchen.

Cut out some cardboard cookies.

Use ice cream tub lids as baking trays.

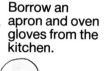

Teddy bear's bed

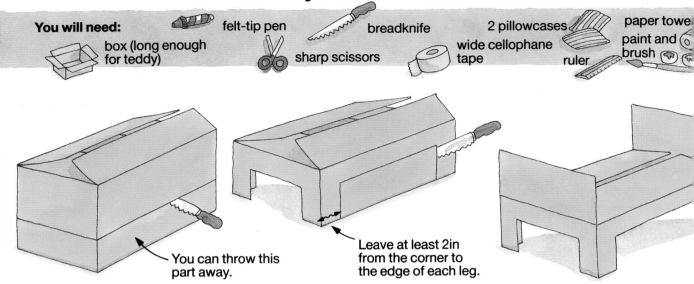

You will need: felt-tip pen • box (long enough for teddy) • sharp scissors • breadknife • wide cellophane tape • 2 pillowcases • ruler • paper towel • paint and brush

You can throw this part away.

Leave at least 2in from the corner to the edge of each leg.

Place the box so you have the flaps at the top. Decide how high you want the bed, draw a line around the bottom and cut off the excess with a breadknife.

Draw and cut rectangular panels from each side, to give the bed four sturdy legs.

Open out the flaps. Fold the longest flaps back into place, leaving the end flaps free.

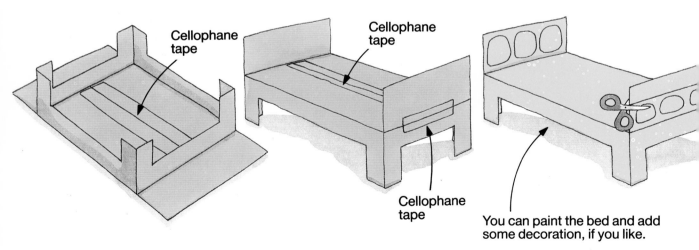

Cellophane tape

Cellophane tape

Cellophane tape

You can paint the bed and add some decoration, if you like.

Turn the bed over and tape the long flaps securely into place underneath.

Turn it upright again and stick tape down the center, and at each end to hold the end flaps upright.

Cut off one end flap to about two thirds of the height of the other and then round off the corners.

20

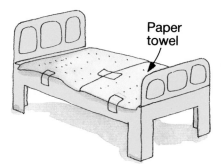 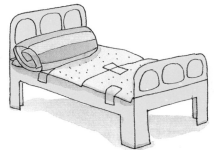 

Paper towel

Use a paper towel lightly taped onto the bed for a bottom sheet.

For the pillow, fold a pillowcase so that it fits the head end of the bed.

Use a second pillowcase as a blanket. Turn back the top.

Other idea to try

Hospital

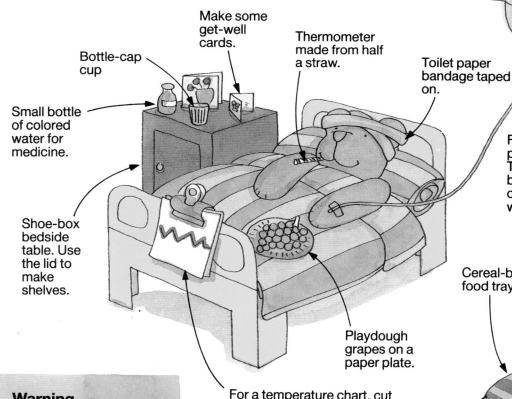

Make some get-well cards.

Bottle-cap cup

Thermometer made from half a straw.

Toilet paper bandage taped on.

Small bottle of colored water for medicine.

For a drip, tape a small plastic bottle to a door. Tape some string to the bottle and attach the other end to teddy's arm with adhesive bandage.

Shoe-box bedside table. Use the lid to make shelves.

Cereal-box food tray.

Playdough grapes on a paper plate.

For a temperature chart, cut some white paper squares. Attach them to the bed end with a paperclip or bulldog clip. Draw a zig-zag line across the paper.

Warning

Don't use candy for pills as this might tempt children to try eating real pills.

Doll's playhouse

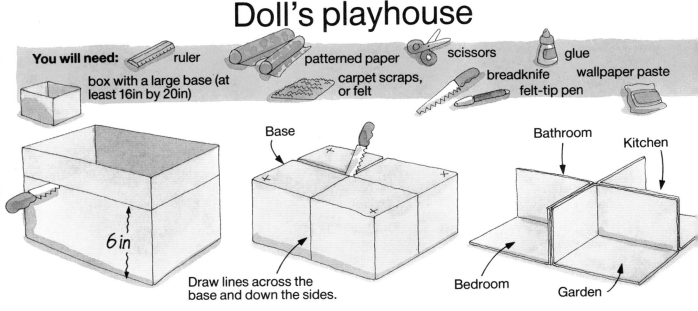

You will need: ruler • patterned paper • scissors • glue
box with a large base (at least 16in by 20in) • carpet scraps, or felt • breadknife • wallpaper paste • felt-tip pen

Base

Bathroom   Kitchen

6 in

Draw lines across the base and down the sides.

Bedroom   Garden

Using a ruler and a felt-tip, measure and mark a line all the way round the box, at least 6in up from the base. Cut around the line with a breadknife.

Turn the box over and mark each corner with a cross. Measure and mark the box into quarters. Cut the box into four sections with a breadknife.

Keep the sections separate to decorate them. Then fit them together with the crosses in the center underneath, long sides against long sides.

To paper your rooms

To carpet your rooms

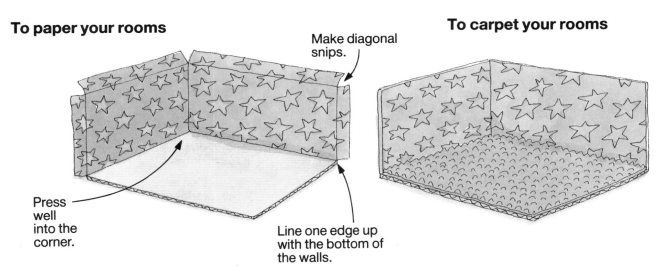

Make diagonal snips.

Press well into the corner.

Line one edge up with the bottom of the walls.

Cut a piece of paper longer and wider than the two walls of your room. Cover the back of the paper with wallpaper paste and glue it to the walls.

Make snips at the edges as shown. Fold the overlaps over and stick them down to make neat edges.

Trim carpet scraps or pieces of felt, or patterned paper, to the right size. Stick them down with glue.

22

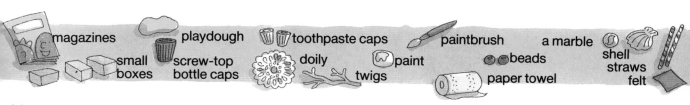
Here and on the next page are some ideas for decorating your rooms.

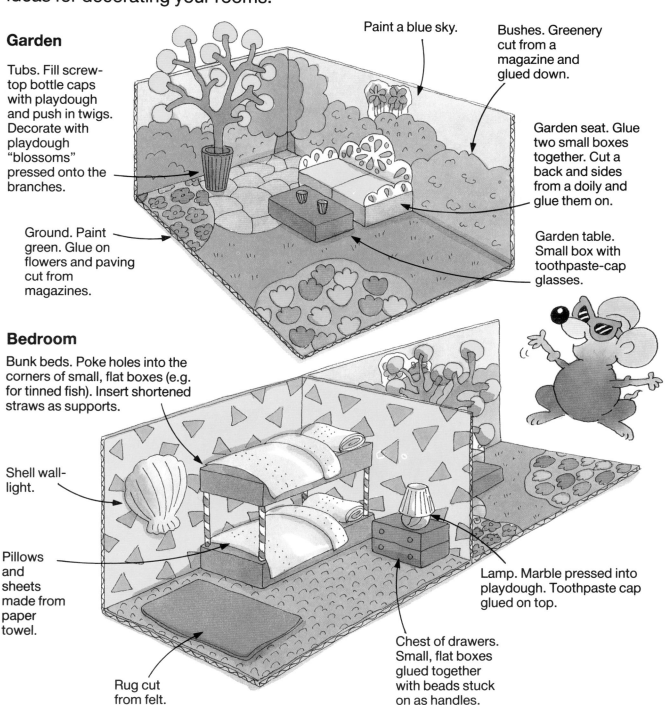

Garden

Tubs. Fill screw-top bottle caps with playdough and push in twigs. Decorate with playdough "blossoms" pressed onto the branches.

Ground. Paint green. Glue on flowers and paving cut from magazines.

Paint a blue sky.

Bushes. Greenery cut from a magazine and glued down.

Garden seat. Glue two small boxes together. Cut a back and sides from a doily and glue them on.

Garden table. Small box with toothpaste-cap glasses.

Bedroom

Bunk beds. Poke holes into the corners of small, flat boxes (e.g. for tinned fish). Insert shortened straws as supports.

Shell wall-light.

Pillows and sheets made from paper towel.

Rug cut from felt.

Lamp. Marble pressed into playdough. Toothpaste cap glued on top.

Chest of drawers. Small, flat boxes glued together with beads stuck on as handles.

23

magazines · matchbox · playdough · scrap of material · straw · bottle caps (screw-on and flat)

small margarine tub · coffee jar lid · felt-tip pen · plastic tub lid · small boxes

cardboard · tinfoil · thin sponge · cellophane tape · toilet paper tubes · yarn

Bathroom

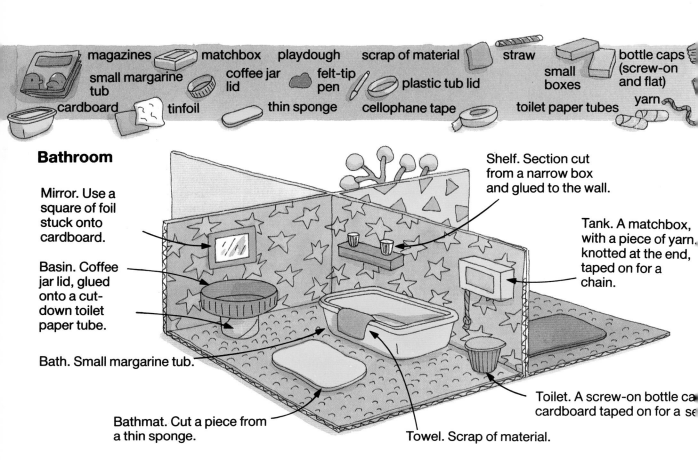

Mirror. Use a square of foil stuck onto cardboard.

Basin. Coffee jar lid, glued onto a cut-down toilet paper tube.

Bath. Small margarine tub.

Bathmat. Cut a piece from a thin sponge.

Shelf. Section cut from a narrow box and glued to the wall.

Tank. A matchbox, with a piece of yarn, knotted at the end, taped on for a chain.

Toilet. A screw-on bottle ca[...] cardboard taped on for a se[...]

Towel. Scrap of material.

Kitchen

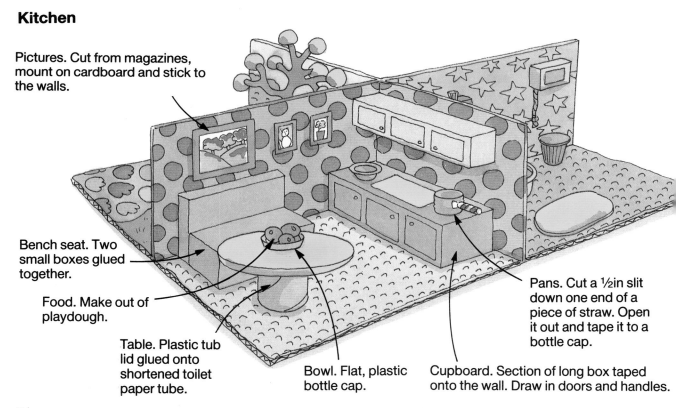

Pictures. Cut from magazines, mount on cardboard and stick to the walls.

Bench seat. Two small boxes glued together.

Food. Make out of playdough.

Table. Plastic tub lid glued onto shortened toilet paper tube.

Bowl. Flat, plastic bottle cap.

Pans. Cut a ½in slit down one end of a piece of straw. Open it out and tape it to a bottle cap.

Cupboard. Section of long box taped onto the wall. Draw in doors and handles.

24

Throw-and-catch games

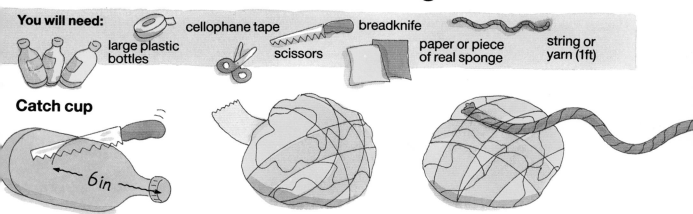
You will need: cellophane tape, large plastic bottles, scissors, breadknife, paper or piece of real sponge, string or yarn (1ft)

Catch cup

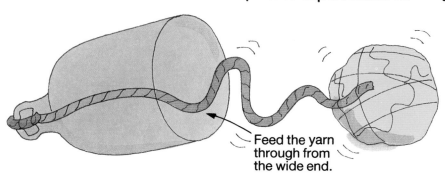

Using a breadknife, cut off a large plastic bottle.

Crumple a piece of paper into a small ball. Wind cellophane tape round it.

Tape a piece of string or yarn, about 1ft long, to the ball.

Feed the yarn through from the wide end.

Remove the bottle cap. Feed the yarn through the bottle and tape the end to the outside of the bottle neck.

Put the ball inside the bottle and then see how many times you can toss it up in the air and catch it again.

Bottle scoopers

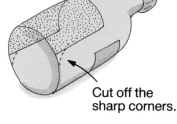

Cut off the sharp corners.

Cut off a large plastic bottle so that it measures about 10in from the neck end.

Using scissors, cut out a section, as shown above. Round off the corners for safety.

Make another scoop and use them to throw and catch a paper ball between two people.

Guessing box

You will need:  food tin (unopened) · kitchen cloth or other light material · felt-tip pen · scissors · shoe box · ruler · cellophane tape · breadknife · various small objects

Cut a rectangle out of one of the small sides of a shoe box.

Put a tin in the middle of the opposite end. Draw around it, using a felt-tip pen.

Push the point of a breadknife into the center of the circle. Cut outward to the edge and then around the circle.

Make sure you can fit your hand inside.

Using the tin as a guide, cut a rectangle of material big enough to cover the circle easily. Cut it in half up the center.

Cut up here.

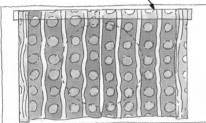

Tape along the top and down the sides.

Tape the material to the inside of the box so that it covers the hole. Replace the box lid.

How to play

One person, the "chooser", chooses a variety of small objects, keeping them out of sight of the "guesser".

The "chooser" puts one of the objects into the box through the rectangular hole. The "guesser" puts a hand through the material to feel the mystery object and tries to guess what it is.

Hints

Try to vary the size, shape and texture of the objects as much as possible.

Don't use sharp or prickly objects.

Other ideas to try

Memory box

Put several things inside the box and remove the lid so the guesser can take a good look.

Put the lid back on, then remove one object without the guesser seeing.

Take the lid off again and see if the guesser can tell what's missing.

Tasting box

Put a variety of foods on saucers. The guesser dips a wet finger into each food in the box, and tastes it with his eyes closed.

Blow football

You will need: yogurt cup • box or lid at least 12in by 18in • cellophane tape • green paint • paint-brush • ruler • felt-tip pen • scissors • breadknife • mug • 2 straws • handful of dried peas

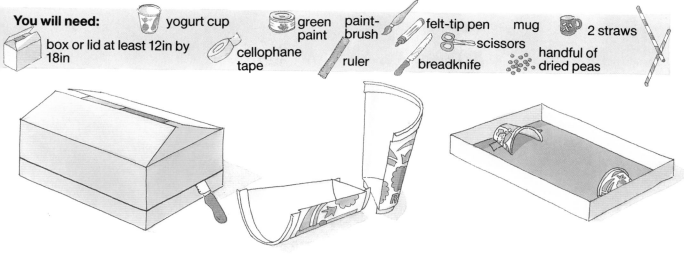

If you are using a box, cut around the base with a breadknife, 2½in from the bottom, to make a tray.

Cut a yogurt cup in half, as shown above, using scissors.

Paint the field green. Tape the yogurt cup halves at either end to make goals.

How to play

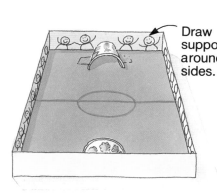

Draw supporters around the sides.

Draw a halfway line using a ruler and felt-tip pen. Draw around a mug to make a center circle.

Put a handful of dried peas into the center circle.

Each player has a straw and uses it to try to blow as many peas as possible into the opposite goal.

The game is over when all the peas are in goal. Count them to find out who is the winner.

Another idea to try

Throw ball

Mark a line on the floor with a piece of yarn. Throw crumpled paper balls into a propped-up box from behind the line.

27

Nodding elephant

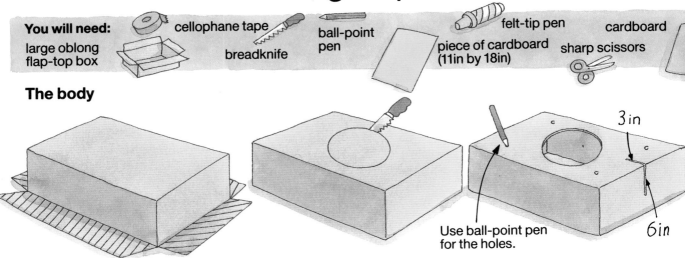

You will need:
large oblong flap-top box — cellophane tape — breadknife — ball-point pen — piece of cardboard (11in by 18in) — felt-tip pen — sharp scissors — cardboard

The body

Turn the box over and cut off the flaps with a breadknife.

Cut a circle in the center top, large enough to fit around your child's waist.

Cut a slit along the top and down the front, as shown. Poke four holes in the top for straps.

Use ball-point pen for the holes.

3 in

6 in

The head

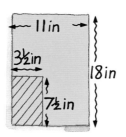

Cut a rectangle 3½in by 7½in from the corner of a large piece of cardboard.

Cut out this part.

Round off the corners with scissors. Draw in a trunk and cut it out.

Draw around the end of a paper towel tube to make two circles, as shown above.

Cut slits from the centers to very slightly beyond the edges.

Push the paper towel tube through the top hole to make handles.

Tape on two cardboard egg box sections for eyes.

Cut two tusks out of the cardboard-box flaps and glue them onto the head.

paper towel
tube

toilet paper tube

ruler

glue

2 sections from
cardboard egg box

continued on
next page

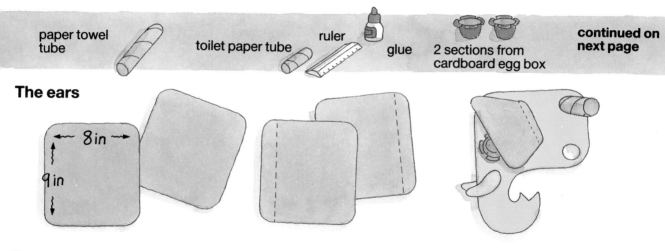

The ears

← 8 in →

9 in

Cut two rectangles out
of cardboard. Round
off the corners, using
scissors.

Make a fold down one
long side of each
rectangle, 1½in from
the edge.

Put some glue along
the folds and stick the
ears onto each side of
the head between the
eye and the handle.

Joining the head and body

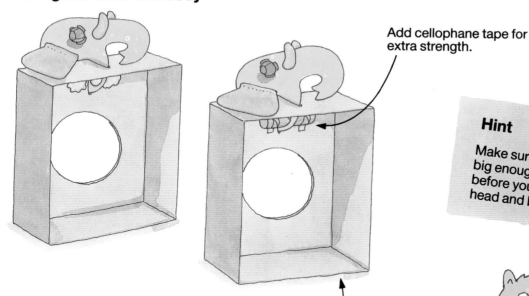

Add cellophane tape for
extra strength.

Hint

Make sure the hole is
big enough for the tube
before you attach the
head and body together.

Put plenty of glue on
either side of the front
slit of the body box, on
the inside of the box.
   Push the head
through the slit from
the outside, so that the
hole in the head is on
the inside.

Stand the box on
end while you
attach the head.

Push a toilet paper
tube through the hole
and press it firmly
against the glued area.

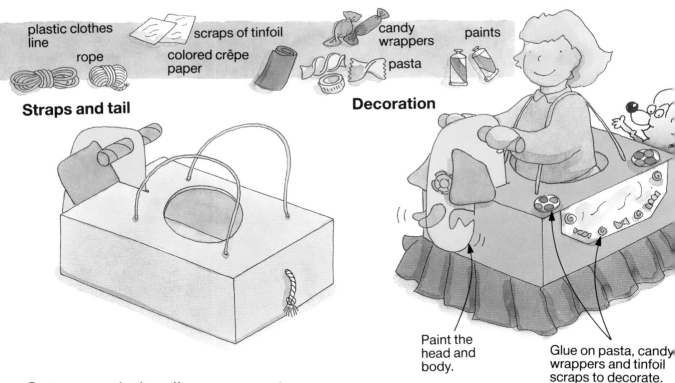

plastic clothes line

rope

scraps of tinfoil

colored crêpe paper

candy wrappers

pasta

paints

Straps and tail

Decoration

Paint the head and body.

Glue on pasta, candy wrappers and tinfoil scraps to decorate.

Cut some clothes line or rope straps the right length to fit over the wearer's shoulders. Thread them through the holes and knot them inside.

Make a hole for a tail with a ball-point pen. Thread some rope through and knot it inside. Knot and fray the end.

Cut a strip of crêpe paper about 8in wide to go around the lower edge of the elephant's body. Attach it with cellophane tape. Stretch the lower edge between your hands to make a frilled effect.

Other ideas to try

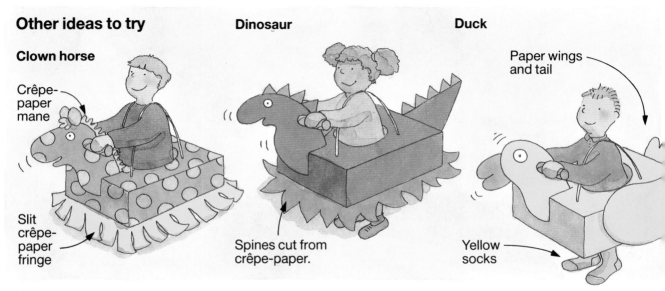

Clown horse

Crêpe-paper mane

Slit crêpe-paper fringe

Dinosaur

Spines cut from crêpe-paper.

Duck

Paper wings and tail

Yellow socks

On this page and the following one you will find some general advice about the equipment and materials needed for the projects in this book, and ways of handling them. The specific things you will need for each project are listed at the top of each page. It is a good idea to collect them all together before you start work.

Work with your child, explaining each stage of your project as you set about it, referring to the pictures and discussing the materials. The process of making the things is just as important as the end result. There will be parts of some of the projects that are too difficult or dangerous for children to do themselves, but they can still learn a lot from watching and helping you.

Some of the projects towards the end of the book will take a little longer than the earlier ones. You will probably want to do them in two or three sessions, rather than all at once. Explain this to your child before you start.

Basic equipment

For nearly all the projects you will need the following:

- Scissors – for cutting paper and thin cardboard. Round-ended with metal blades for children and, occasionally, sharp-ended for adults only.

- Knife – for cutting thick cardboard. The best type to use is a breadknife or other sturdy knife with a serrated edge. For adults only.

- Felt-tip pen – for marking lines to cut along.

- Ball-point pen – for making holes in cardboard.

- Ruler – for measuring.

- Pencil

- Glue

- Cellophane tape

Finding your materials

You can collect nearly all of the materials you will need by saving the packaging from your everyday shopping. The lists below will help you to spot the sort of things that will come in handy.

Cardboard boxes and cartons for:

cereal (a good source of thin cardboard)

tea bags and loose tea

soap

soap powder

toothpaste tubes

sardines

eggs

cookies

matches

shoes

milk and juice

pizzas

Plastic containers for:

shampoos and conditioners

soft drinks

yogurt

margarine

spreads

ice cream

clothes-washing liquid

dishwashing liquid

Polystyrene:
food trays pizza bases

Lids and caps (metal or plastic) for:

bottles (flat and screw-topped)

jam-jars

toothpaste tubes

margarine and yogurt tubs

liquid soaps

Cardboard tubes for:

toilet paper

paper towel

wrapping paper

It is also worth saving a few other everyday odds and ends:

Paper:

wrapping paper from flowers or presents

left-over wallpaper

old magazines

candy wrappers

tissue paper

crêpe paper

Things for tying and threading:

laces

yarn

string

rope

plastic clothes line

Things from your kitchen

paper towels

tinfoil

plastic wrap (use the microwave variety if possible – it is thicker and less fly-away)

disposable cleaning cloths

thin mopping-up sponges

paper and plastic plates and cups

straws

Asking at shops

Some of the projects require fairly large cardboard boxes. Grocery stores or supermarkets can normally let you have a selection of flap-top boxes. For really large boxes ask at electrical stores that sell refrigerators, washing machines etc.

Shoe shops usually have some unwanted, empty shoe boxes and candy shops may be able to give you large, empty, plastic jars.

Cleaning your materials

Wash things like yogurt cups and bottle caps before using them and wipe paper plates with a damp cloth. Make sure anything you use is thoroughly dry, however, before using glue or cellophane tape on it.

It is a good idea to sterilize some things before use e.g. polystyrene food trays, which are porous and may have held meat. Buy a sterilizing solution from a drugstore and follow the instructions. Then, rinse and dry thoroughly before use.

Cutting cardboard

Children who are fairly competent at cutting paper with scissors may be able to cope with cutting thin cardboard, but it is quite tiring on the hand and they will probably need help.

The best way of cutting thick cardboard and large boxes is to use a breadknife as though it were a saw – the downward stroke away from you should have the most pressure. Make it clear to young children that they should not try to do this themselves and keep the knife out of reach. Make sure your child stands well back when you are sawing.

When cutting the top or bottom section off a box, start by sawing across a corner, then insert the blade and continue.

To cut into a flat surface, first insert the point of a ball-point pen to make a small hole for the blade of the knife to fit into.

Turn the box as you cut, so that the area you are cutting is always at the top. This will give you greater control.

Sticking

●Wallpaper paste. This is good for large areas but is not very strong. For safety always use the non-fungicidal kind. You can store left-over paste in the refrigerator, covered with plastic wrap.

●PVA (polyvinyl acetate) glues. These are also good for large areas. They are available from hardware stores. Apply the glue with a brush. It is white but dries transparent. Protect clothing and wash brushes after use.

●Strong glue. For some jobs, such as sticking yogurt cups or bottle caps onto cardboard, you need to use a fairly strong glue. Buy a tube of non-toxic glue from a hardware store. Do not use solvent-based or instant-bond glues.

●Colored cellophane tape. This is good for decoration if you want stripes or patterns.

Painting

Use powder paints or liquid poster paints. Powder paint is cheaper but tends to be thinner. You can thicken it by mixing it with wallpaper paste, flour and water paste, PVA glue or soapflakes. If you mix a little liquid soap into the paint, it will wash off furniture and clothes more easily. For painting large areas, use small adult-sized brushes.